# HEROES
## OF
# THE YEAR

Extraordinary Ernie
& Marvelous Maud

HEROES
OF
THE YEAR

Frances Watts
Illustrated by Judy Watson

Eerdmans Books for Young Readers
Grand Rapids, Michigan / Cambridge, U.K.

Text © 2011 Frances Watts
Illustrations © 2011 Judy Watson

First published 2011 in Australia by
HarperCollins*Publishers* Australia Pty Limited

This edition published 2012 in the United States of America by
Eerdmans Books for Young Readers,
an imprint of Wm. B. Eerdmans Publishing Co.
2140 Oak Industrial Dr. NE, Grand Rapids, Michigan 49505
P.O. Box 163, Cambridge CB3 9PU U.K.

www.eerdmans.com/youngreaders

Manufactured at Versa Press, East Peoria, Illinois, USA,
in February 2012; first printing

12 13 14 15 16 17 18    7 6 5 4 3 2 1

Library of Congress Cataloging-in-Publication Data

Watts, Frances.
Heroes of the Year / by Frances Watts; illustrated by Judy Watson.
p. cm.
Summary: Extraordinary Ernie and Marvelous Maud,
the ten-year-old superhero-in-training and his sidekick sheep,
have a good chance of winning the Heroes of the Year award
until a pencil-wielding fiend starts to wreak havoc in the town of Baxter.
ISBN 978-0-8028-5412-4
[1. Superheroes — Fiction. 2. Sheep — Fiction. 3. Contests — Fiction.]
I. Watson, Judy, 1959- ill. II. Title.
PZ7.W3355Her 2012
[Fic] — dc23
2011042738

For Kerry and Rod, who look great in mustaches.
— *F.W.*


For my sons,
Amazing Arthur and Heroic Hugo,
and for my friends
Courageous Kerrie and Terrific Tom.
Keep on making the world a better
and more beautiful place!
— *J.W.*

# ONE

Ernie Eggers strode down Main Street on Monday afternoon, his long green cape swishing behind him and the heels of his tall black boots echoing loudly as they struck the pavement. Usually the serious sound his footsteps made when he was wearing his big boots filled Ernie with pleasure, but not today. He'd just come from his school sports carnival, and as usual he hadn't won a single ribbon. Today his footsteps tapped out the word "lo-ser, lo-ser."

Ernie glanced at the town hall clock as he passed. Five to four — he was right on time.

Then he glanced again. Something seemed a little odd about the town hall. He ran his eyes over the white building. There were the double doors, above them was the giant portrait of the mayor, and above that the clock tower (which told him it was now four minutes to four). There was nothing out of place.

Shaking his head, he turned and continued down the street, past the pharmacy, the bank, the pet store, and the laundromat, to number 32, the headquarters of the Superheroes Society (Baxter Branch). The windows of the Superheroes Society were covered as usual, but no longer with an assortment of yellowing pages from old newspapers. Instead, every inch of glass was plastered with posters. In the top left-hand corner of each poster was the face of Super Whiz, looking intelligent and important. The rest of the poster was taken up with a giant picture of a yellow book with the words *100 Handy Hints for Heroing* printed in bright red across the cover. There was another poster stuck on the shabby brown door.

Ernie admired the posters for a minute, then

turned as he caught a flutter of pink — and was that a flash of red? — from the corner of his eye. A sheep in a short pink cape was trotting up the street from the direction of the park.

"Hi, partner," said Maud a bit breathlessly as she reached number 32. "I had to run to get here in time. My gymnastics class doesn't finish till quarter to four. I didn't even have time to change out of my leotard."

A gust of wind swept her pink cape aloft

and Ernie saw that the red costume beneath was indeed a leotard.

As the town hall clock struck four, Ernie checked his reflection in the window of the laundromat, making sure that the legs of his green one-piece suit were tucked neatly into his boots and that the arms, with the gold lightning bolts on the sleeves, were straight. "Ready to get to work?"

Maud tugged at her pink cape with her teeth until it was arranged neatly across her back. "I sure am," she said.

It had been many months now since Ernie had won the competition to become a trainee superhero with the Superheroes Society (Baxter Branch) and met his sidekick, Maud. Since then, Extraordinary Ernie and Marvelous Maud had been patrolling Main Street on Monday, Tuesday, and Thursday afternoons and all day Saturday, stamping out Mischief and Mayhem, and putting a halt to Havoc.

As they strolled past the florist, in the direction of the park, Ernie said, "So you're doing

gymnastics now? What about your art classes?"

Maud shook her woolly head. "I'm not taking them anymore."

"But, Maud, you loved your art classes," said Ernie. "And you're so talented." One of Maud's paintings hung on his bedroom wall at home. The picture of Ernie with his hero, The Daring Dynamo, was one of his most prized possessions.

Maud smiled at Ernie's praise. "Thanks, Ernie," she said. "But while art is a wonderful hobby, I've been thinking that I'd like to do something to improve myself professionally. At first I couldn't decide between yogurt and gymnastics, but in the end I decided that gymnastics would be more useful for my work as a sidekick."

"Um, what's the difference?" Ernie asked.

"Yogurt's more about stretching," Maud explained as they looked both ways then crossed the street into the park. "But imagine how useful I'll be if I'm a sidekick *and* a gymnast. The vault will improve my leaping, and the balance beam will improve my balance, and doing the splits will improve my flexibility."

"You can do the splits?" said Ernie. "Wow!"

Maud hung her head. "I can't actually do the splits," she confessed. "Not yet." Then she brightened. "But I'm great at vaulting. All sheep are. I think it comes from jumping so many fences."

Ernie sighed. "You're lucky to be a natural athlete, Maud. We had our school sports carnival today, and I didn't win a single ribbon. I never do. I thought it would be different this year, now that I'm a trainee superhero, but . . ." Ernie lifted his shoulders then let them drop again. He remembered how Lenny Pascal, who had won

three ribbons, had called him "Super Slowcoach" and everyone had laughed.

"Oh, that's too bad, Ernie," said Maud sympathetically. "Did you come in last?"

"No," said Ernie. "In one race I came in fourth. That was the best I did."

"Well, fourth is pretty good. Where did you come in last year?"

"Last year?" Ernie thought for a moment. "Eighth," he said finally.

"You went from eighth to fourth in a single year? That's fantastic, partner!" Maud exclaimed. "If you keep improving that quickly, you'll definitely get a ribbon next year."

"You're right," said Ernie. He hadn't looked at it like that. All of a sudden he felt less glum.

They were busy in the park for some time, picking up the trash some careless picnickers had left behind, and helping some lost ducklings find their mother. It was almost five o'clock by the time they walked back up Main Street toward the town hall.

As they approached the end of the block,

Ernie was reminded of his earlier feeling.

"Maud," he said, "does the town hall look different to you?"

Maud tilted her head to one side and considered the white building. "It looks the same as it always does," she said.

Ernie shook his head in frustration. "I can't put my finger on it, but — Hang on . . ." He moved closer until he was standing at the foot of the double doors. "Look! The mayor has a mustache!"

Maud squinted at the portrait of the mayor. "Hasn't she always had one?"

"No," said Ernie definitely. "Some mischief-maker or wrongdoer has drawn that mustache on. Quick, we'd better go tell the others!" And he took off down Main Street at a run.

# TWO

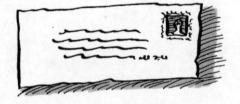

Ernie burst through the shabby brown door of 32 Main Street to find Super Whiz standing at the head of the long table in the middle of the room. At first, Ernie thought the president must be reading from his new book, but when he looked at the other superheroes of Baxter Branch he changed his mind.

Valiant Vera and Amazing Desmond were sitting on opposite sides of the table, looking up at Super Whiz.

"Go on, Whiz," Desmond was saying. "Keep reading."

Ernie had never heard Amazing Desmond encourage Super Whiz to keep reading anything, except perhaps a pizza menu. And whatever Super Whiz was reading was so exciting, the president didn't even stop to complain about Desmond calling him Whiz (which he hated).

Even Housecat Woman, who was curled up in her usual armchair, had both eyes open and fixed on the president of the Superheroes Society (Baxter Branch).

"The Heroes of the Year will be chosen from among the trainees —"

"Wait," said Valiant Vera, catching sight of Ernie and Maud in the doorway. "Here are Ernie and Maud now."

"Ah, excellent," said Super Whiz, lowering the piece of paper he was holding. "Patrol went well, I trust?"

"Someone has — " Ernie began, pointing in the direction of the town hall.

"Of course it went well," Super Whiz continued, before Ernie could finish. "Our trainees' patrols *always* go well." He looked around the

room thoughtfully. "We'll probably need to build a trophy shelf."

A trophy shelf? What was going on?

"Come over here, you two," Amazing Desmond said, beckoning. "Whiz has received a very important letter from the Superheroes Society National Headquarters."

"Is it about *100 Handy Hints for Heroing*?" Ernie asked eagerly, slipping into a seat beside Valiant Vera as Maud took her place alongside Desmond. "Has it won a prize?"

"No, no, not the book," said Super Whiz. "This is something that affects you two."

"Us?" said Maud. "Is it something good?"

"It might be," said Vera, smiling. "It's a competition."

"Oh," said Ernie. He'd hoped that maybe The Daring Dynamo was coming to visit, or that there might be another picture of him and Maud in the Superheroes Society newsletter. But a competition . . . ? After the school sports carnival, Ernie had had enough of competitions. Whatever it was, he was bound to lose. Or come in fourth.

"Extraordinary Ernie," Super Whiz said, "and Marvelous Maud . . . how would you like to be the Superheroes Society's Heroes of the Year?"

"Heroes of the Year?" exclaimed Maud. "That would be great!"

"Yeah," said Ernie, without much enthusiasm. "Great."

"Come on, Whiz," Amazing Desmond urged. "Read the letter."

Super Whiz brought the paper back up to his nose. "I'll start from the beginning," he said. "Dear Superheroes: The Superheroes Society National Headquarters is delighted to announce that, due to the high caliber of trainee superheroes noted at last month's National Superheroes Conference, we will once again be awarding a prize to the Heroes of the Year."

"When was the prize last awarded, Vera?" Amazing Desmond asked. "Can you remember?"

Vera shook her head. "This will be the first one in years and years," she replied. "I can't even remember how long ago it was that we won."

Ernie's mouth dropped open. "You were the

Heroes of the Year?" he said.

"Oh yes," said Vera. "Look." She pointed to a framed photo hanging on the wall.

Ernie turned his head to study the old photo of four young superheroes gathered around an enormous gold trophy. He had walked past the photo dozens of times, but had never really looked at it before. Now, despite the faded colors, he could identify a much younger Super Whiz in his blue costume with the red SW stamped across the front, and Valiant Vera in pink and gold. There was Amazing Desmond,

his orange top and purple tights clinging to a slim, muscular frame. As for Housecat Woman, Ernie didn't think he would have recognized her if she hadn't been wearing her familiar black costume.

"Look at Housecat Woman," Vera said fondly. "She was only a kitten."

Housecat Woman stretched and yawned. "I was a bundle of energy in those days," she agreed sleepily.

Ernie's eyes were drawn back to the center of the photo. "That trophy," he said. "Is that — is that what the Heroes of the Year get?" His mouth had turned dry. A ribbon was one thing, but a trophy? A trophy was better than a ribbon . . . A trophy was better than three ribbons! "I've never won a trophy before," he added shyly.

"Where is our trophy, anyway?" Vera asked.

All the superheroes looked around the room. The only thing that seemed vaguely trophy-like was a dusty old cup on top of the fridge with a long-dead bunch of flowers in it. "It's not that, is it?" Ernie asked.

"Oh dear," said Vera, shaking her head in dismay. "That's no way to treat our history."

"Ahem!" said Super Whiz, clearing his throat. He waved the paper in his hand to attract their attention, then continued reading.

"Starting next week, the judges will begin touring the country on secret inspections, observing trainee superheroes in action and assessing their standing in the local community. The Heroes of the Year will be chosen from among the trainees and a gold trophy awarded to the winning branch."

Super Whiz put the letter on the table and sat down. "Superheroes of Baxter Branch," he said, "as your president I tell you this: we will win that trophy. Extraordinary Ernie and Marvelous Maud will be Heroes of the Year!"

"And when they win," Amazing Desmond

added, "we'll celebrate with a big party and lots of pizza. You know what they say: winners are pizza eaters."

Valiant Vera gave him a puzzled look. "I think you mean winners are grinners," she corrected.

Desmond shook his head. "No," he said. "Pizza eaters are grinners." He leaned backward in his chair and plucked the menu of Ronald's Super-Terrific Pizza Parlor from under a fridge magnet.

He gave the menu to Ernie. "Read this aloud,"

he ordered.

"Margherita," Ernie read obediently.

Amazing Desmond smiled.

"Ham and pineapple," Ernie read.

Amazing Desmond beamed.

"Super-Triple-Supremo Supreme with extra cheese and pepperoni."

Amazing Desmond's face split into a giant grin. "See?" he said. "That's what a winner looks like!"

Valiant Vera frowned at him, but Ernie could tell she was trying not to laugh.

"Amazing Desmond," Super Whiz said sternly.

"Yes, Whiz?" said Desmond, turning his grin on the president.

"We have a lot of work ahead of us if we are to win this competition, so we need to be serious and focused, do you understand? And don't call me Whiz."

"Yes, Whiz," said Desmond. He winked at Ernie, then adopted a serious face.

"Okay, everyone," said Super Whiz, drumming his fingers on the table, "we need a plan."

He held his chin in his hand and looked at the ceiling. "A strategy . . ."

"A scheme," Amazing Desmond chimed in.

"Do you really think that's necessary?" Valiant Vera asked. "Surely if Ernie and Maud keep on doing the same excellent job they've been doing for the last few months, the judges are bound to be impressed. Why, when we were at the conference last month, everyone congratulated us on the quality of our trainees."

Ernie and Maud exchanged smiles, and Ernie knew that Maud, too, was remembering how the crowd had cheered for them after they captured the villainous Chicken George, who had turned out to be not such a villain after all . . .

Suddenly Ernie clapped a hand to his mouth. Thinking of villains had reminded him of what they had seen while on patrol. "Someone has drawn a mustache on the portrait of the mayor!" he blurted out.

"A mustache?" Super Whiz demanded.

"On the mayor?" gasped Valiant Vera.

"Didn't she always have one?" said Desmond.

Super Whiz looked at Valiant Vera. "Surely it couldn't be . . ."

Valiant Vera nodded slowly. "I'm afraid it could," she said. "When we were at the conference, Magnificent Marjory mentioned that the fiend had passed through Beezerville and wreaked havoc. There were mustaches drawn all over town. I'm afraid it's him, all right."

"Who?" asked Maud. "Who are you talking about?"

Valiant Vera looked grave. "Pencil Pete," she said.

# THREE

After school on Tuesday, Ernie rushed home to change into his superhero costume, then raced down to Main Street. Glancing at the town hall clock, and then at the mustachioed mayor, he knew it was more important than ever to be punctual, with Pencil Pete on the loose.

Pencil Pete had been traveling all over the country, drawing mustaches on every poster and billboard in his path — and though many super-heroes had tried, none had succeeded in catching him. And now he was in Baxter. Ernie shivered. He and Maud would have to be super alert if they were to prevent him from doing any more damage around their town.

"Hi, Maud," he said as his sidekick clattered up to join him outside the shabby brown door of number 32. "You didn't see any more mustaches on your way here, did you?"

Maud shook her head. "No." Then she added in a hopeful voice, "Maybe Pencil Pete has left Baxter already."

They set off up Main Street in the direction of the town hall. Ernie was pleased to note that there was no sign of Pencil Pete anywhere. He began to relax.

"How are your gymnastics classes going?" he asked his sidekick.

"Well, I'm very good at the balance beam," said Maud. "My gymnastics teacher said she's never seen a sheep with such fine balance."

It seemed to Ernie that Maud didn't sound as happy about this as she should have. "That's good, isn't it?" he said.

"Oh, Ernie," Maud wailed. "I still can't do the splits. At first my teacher said it was just a matter of practice, but I practiced all day yesterday and I can only get halfway down."

"You'll get there, Maud," Ernie said.

"I don't know, Ernie." Maud sounded discouraged.

They had just reached the supermarket on their second lap of the shops when Ernie saw it . . . Up on a billboard, someone had drawn a giant mustache on the lady advertising laundry detergent! And Ernie was sure it hadn't been there when they'd last passed it.

"Maud," he said, "Pencil Pete has been here!"

"Ernie, look!" said his partner. She was pointing her hoof at a small man in a blue suit running down Main Street. In his hand was a giant pencil.

"After him!" said Ernie.

Ernie broke into a run, Maud trotting along beside him. Past the bookstore, the newsstand, and the convenience store they sprinted, Maud slightly in front, but as they drew level with the fruit shop Ernie saw that a customer had bumped into the banana display, and the fruit was scattered in their path. "Maud, be careful — bananas!"

It was too late. With a squelch, Maud ran straight into the spilled bananas.

"Whoooaaaa!" she cried as she skidded wildly along the pavement, a banana peel under each hoof.

"I'm coming, Maud!" Carefully dodging the remaining bananas, Ernie took off in pursuit.

Maud had just sailed past the toyshop when Ernie heard a child's shriek. It had come from a little girl; the wind had blown her balloon right out of her hand. Her father, his arms full of groceries, was looking on helplessly.

"Don't worry," Ernie told the little girl as they passed her. "We'll get your balloon back . . . Maud! The balloon!"

Maud's cry ceased mid-bleat as she closed her mouth with a snap around the string of the balloon.

Putting on a surge of speed, Ernie grabbed Maud's cape and managed to slow her down so that she slid to a graceful stop.

They both walked back to the little girl, who was happy to be reunited with her balloon. Ernie tied it around her wrist so she wouldn't lose it again.

The little girl's father was very grateful. "I'm going to write a letter to the Superheroes Society telling them what you did here today," he promised.

Maud tugged her cape straight and then she and Ernie continued down the block.

"I'm really glad we helped that little girl," said Ernie. "But we lost Pencil Pete."

Indeed, though they scanned both sides of the street, there was no sign of the man with the giant pencil.

When they got to the park they went straight to the pond so that Maud could wash the squashed banana from her hooves.

"I might be a vegetarian," Maud commented to Ernie as she wiped her hooves dry on the grass, "but I can't *stand* bananas."

"You did a great job of standing *on* them, though," Ernie pointed out. "Your gymnastics teacher is right about your fine balance."

As they headed back up Main Street, Ernie said, "We'd better go tell the others about Pencil Pete." But as they reached number 32, Ernie stared in horror at the sight of the poster on the door.

The Super Whiz on the poster now had a long, curling mustache.

Ernie threw open the door and called to the superheroes inside, "Pencil Pete has struck again!"

Super Whiz rushed outside, followed by Valiant Vera.

"This . . . this is outrageous!" Super Whiz was trembling with fury. He stormed back inside. "He must be stopped, he must be —" Super Whiz drew to a halt so abruptly that Ernie almost ran into him.

Then Ernie saw what Super Whiz was looking at: Amazing Desmond was standing in front of a poster on the wall with a pencil in his hand.

"DESMOND!" Super Whiz roared.

"Oops!" Amazing Desmond dropped the pencil. "Now look what you've made me do." A penciled line on the poster ran from beneath Super Whiz's nose all the way down to his chin.

Ernie was aghast. "*You're* Pencil Pete?" he said to Amazing Desmond.

Desmond laughed. "Of course not," he replied.

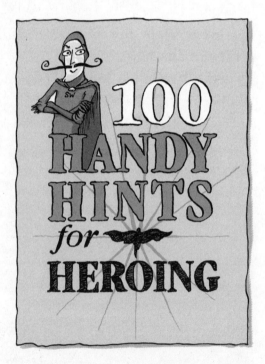

"Though Pencil Pete did give me the idea."

The superheroes gathered around the long table, and Ernie and Maud reported their sighting of Pencil Pete on Main Street.

"But he's still on the loose," Ernie said apologetically.

"Hmmm, he certainly is elusive," Valiant Vera said. "Do you know what we need? We need a plan. Perhaps if we —"

"Wait a minute." Super Whiz, at the head of the table, held up his hand. "We were already in the middle of a planning session." He turned to Ernie and Maud. "We were having a meeting to discuss your strategy for winning the Heroes of the Year award."

"And like I told you," Vera interrupted, "I think you're taking the wrong approach. The Heroes of the Year award is not about strategies. It's not even about winning! It's about how our trainees perform their duties year-round."

Super Whiz sat up straight and threw back his shoulders. "Now, Vera," he said importantly, "as the president of Baxter Branch I really feel it is up to me to determine our policy in this matter. And I'm sure we all agree that winning the Heroes of the Year competition is of the utmost importance — just think of the fame and glory it will bring to our branch."

"A bit of fame and glory might help to turn your book into a bestseller, eh Whiz?" said Desmond.

Super Whiz looked uncomfortable. "Desmond," he said stiffly, "I resent —"

But Desmond was looking at Ernie and Maud. "What do you two think?" he said. "Do you want to be Heroes of the Year?"

Ernie didn't know what to say. Of course he wanted to be a Hero of the Year, but not if it meant Vera and Super Whiz arguing. And what about Pencil Pete? Ernie wanted to hear Valiant Vera's ideas for catching the pencil-wielding villain. He turned to Maud to see what she thought, and as he did he was momentarily blinded by a gleam of gold. There, on a brand-new shelf, was a trophy, glowing in the afternoon sun that poured in through the high dusty window over the front door.

"What's that?" he breathed.

Super Whiz glanced over at the shelf. "Ah, our Heroes of the Year trophy," he said proudly. "We gave our old prize a polish. It cleaned up rather well, didn't it? And when you two win your trophy, we'll put it right next to ours."

Ernie felt something stir inside him as he gazed at the glowing trophy. He could just imagine the look on Lenny Pascal's face when he saw it.

Suddenly, he wanted a golden trophy more than he'd ever wanted anything before.

"Yes," he said to Amazing Desmond loudly, Pencil Pete momentarily forgotten, "I want to be a Hero of the Year. What do we have to do to win?"

"I'll tell you how we win," said Desmond. "It's simple. We find out who the judges are and when they're coming to Baxter, then you two dazzle 'em."

Super Whiz cocked his head to one side. "Desmond," he said, "that's an amazingly good idea."

"I'm not called Amazing for nothing," Desmond agreed.

"But aren't the judges' inspections being done secretly?" Ernie asked.

"Yes," said Vera firmly, "they are." She looked at Maud, and then Ernie. "Listen to me, you two," she said. "You can be Heroes of the Year just by being yourselves."

But although Vera was one of the smartest people Ernie had ever met, he thought she was probably wrong about this. Ernie had been himself his whole life, and no one had ever given him a trophy for it.

# FOUR

When Ernie and Maud did their patrol on Thursday afternoon, Ernie was still thinking about the glowing gold trophy. He tried to think of special skills he had that might impress the judges. When he couldn't come up with any, he thought of Maud's skills instead. Perhaps the Heroes of the Year judges would be impressed by a sheep who could do the splits.

"Can you do the splits yet, Maud?" he asked his partner as they completed a circuit of the park and headed up Main Street.

Maud shook her head. "My teacher said that

maybe the reason I can't do the splits is because I'm a sheep. I'm sick of people always saying that sheep can't do things," she grumbled.

"Ah," said Ernie, thinking once more of the gold trophy on the shelf, "but what if it was a sheep who was *Hero of the Year?*"

Maud's eyes widened. "You're right, Ernie," she said. "A sheep who was Hero of the Year could do *anything*."

They were just passing the convenience store when, up ahead, Mr. Winters, the owner of the newsstand, came running out of his shop clutching a magazine. He looked wildly from left to right then, spotting Ernie and Maud, hurried toward them.

"Thank goodness you're here," he said. "Look at this!" And he thrust the magazine at the two trainee superheroes. It was a copy of *Baxter Belle*, and on the front was a smiling woman with a big mustache.

"A man came in with a big pencil and drew mustaches on every copy of *Baxter Belle* in the shop!" Mr. Winters said. "You have to stop him!"

40

"We'll try," Ernie promised. "Which way did he go?"

Mr. Winters shrugged. "He was gone by the time I got to the door."

"We'll find him," Ernie said, more confidently than he felt. "Don't worry, Mr. Winters."

But although he and Maud jogged up and down both sides of Main Street, and around the park twice, Pencil Pete was nowhere to be seen.

"I can't believe he got away from us again," Ernie groaned, as he and Maud walked back to number 32 to report on their patrol. "Not only did we not catch him, we didn't even catch *sight* of him."

"Maybe he saw us coming," Maud mused, "and that's why he disappeared so quickly. Maybe he's heard how good we are at stopping villains."

✎

Back at headquarters, the superheroes were in the middle of a disagreement.

"We really need to be focusing on Pencil

Pete," Vera was arguing as Ernie and Maud entered. "He's creating chaos in our town!"

"Yes, yes, I see your point, Vera," said Super Whiz, "but one thing at a time. I'm certain that if Ernie and Maud are named Heroes of the Year, Pencil Pete will know he's beaten."

"That's right," said Desmond. "We'll take care of Pencil Pete later. Right now we've got bigger

fish to fry."

"I'm not sure," said Maud doubtfully. "I'm a vegetarian, you know."

"It's okay, Maud," Desmond told her. "We won't really be frying fish. It's just a figure of speech."

"What Desmond is trying to say," Super Whiz explained, "is that your most important task at the moment is impressing the judges and winning the Heroes of the Year award."

Valiant Vera sighed. "Tell me," she said to Ernie and Maud, "why do you want the Heroes of the Year award?"

"The trophy," whispered Ernie guiltily. "I've never won anything like that before."

"I want to prove that sheep can do anything," said Maud in a low voice.

"I can understand that you want to win," said Vera. "It feels good to win. But think about why you want that award. It sounds to me like you each want something for yourselves. Being Heroes of the Year isn't about winning, though. It's about being the best superhero you can be, all the time, every day." She turned to Super Whiz and Desmond. "And you two should know better. You shouldn't be seeing the Heroes of the Year award as an opportunity for fame and glory." She looked at Super Whiz, who reddened with embarrassment. "Or as an opportunity to eat pizza," Valiant Vera said to Amazing Desmond, who looked shame-faced. "This is an opportunity to teach Ernie and Maud about heroing, not winning."

"Everything they need to know about heroing is in my book," Super Whiz protested. "You've read it, haven't you, Ernie? What about you, Maud?"

"Twice," said Ernie.

"Me too," said Maud.

Valiant Vera crossed her arms. "Well, I suggest you all have a good long think about what's really important to the Baxter Branch of the Superheroes Society."

That night, when Ernie climbed into bed, he wasn't thinking about the trophy. He was thinking about Pencil Pete. He had promised Mr. Winters that he would try to stop the pencil-wielding fiend — but he hadn't even remembered to report Pencil Pete's latest act of mischief. The people of Baxter were counting on him, and he had let them down! Valiant Vera had said many times that caring for their community was the single most important duty a superhero had.

But how could Ernie stop Pencil Pete? He needed the help of the other superheroes, he decided. He was only a trainee superhero, after all. There was still so much he didn't know. Then he remembered Super Whiz saying, "Everything they need to know about heroing is in my book."

Ernie jumped out of bed and fetched *100 Handy Hints for Heroing* from his bookshelf. There were

some great hints in the book, Ernie knew. Like number 27: *If your costume includes a long cape, try to walk into the wind wherever possible.* (Ernie, whose cape had blown over his head on more than one occasion, thought this was particularly useful advice.) Or number 46: *Never wash a white cape with a red towel, unless you desire a pink cape.* Or number 73, he thought, as he drifted off to sleep . . .

# FIVE

When Ernie got to the Superheroes Society headquarters on Saturday morning, Maud was already there. Once again she was wearing her red leotard under her cape.

"Hi, Maud," Ernie said. "Did you do gymnastics this morning?" He nodded toward her leotard.

"I got up early to practice the splits some more," Maud said. "But I still can't do them." She hung her head sorrowfully. "I might as well face it: there are some things sheep just can't do."

Ernie thought he knew a way to cheer Maud

up. "I'll tell you something super a sheep *can* do," he said. "Catch Pencil Pete!"

Maud lifted her head hopefully. "Ernie," she said, "do you have a plan?"

"I think so, Maud. At least, I have the beginnings of one. I'd like to ask the superheroes for advice, though."

They pushed open the shabby brown door to find Super Whiz sitting at the head of the long table reading *100 Handy Hints for Heroing*, Amazing Desmond leaning on the fridge reading a pizza menu, and Housecat Woman snoozing in her armchair.

"Hi, everyone. Where's Vera?" Ernie asked.

Desmond looked up. "Hello there, you two. Vera's visiting Magnificent Marjory in Beezerville today. She won't be back till this afternoon."

"Oh." Ernie was disappointed. "Before we start our patrol today, I wanted to tell you all about an idea I had to stop Pencil Pete."

"Really?" Super Whiz put down his book. "That's very interesting. Why don't you sit down?"

Desmond, Ernie, and Maud took their seats

at the long table, and everyone looked at Ernie expectantly.

*"Confound your enemies as a master of disguise,"* he said aloud.

"Hint number 73 in my book," Super Whiz said. "I'm glad to see it has made an impression on you."

"What I mean is," Ernie elaborated, "we could go after Pencil Pete in disguise. You see, Maud made a good point the other day. She said that maybe the reason we couldn't catch Pencil Pete was because he always saw us coming. But if we

were in disguise, he wouldn't recognize us, so he wouldn't run away — and we could catch him."

Super Whiz nodded thoughtfully. "That's a very good idea, Ernie," he said. "But what kind of disguise would you wear?"

Ernie sighed. "That's the bit I need help with," he said. As he looked around the room in search of inspiration, his eyes rested on the poster of Super Whiz and his book. He looked at the mustache Desmond had started to pencil on Super Whiz's picture. Pencil Pete had given him the idea, Desmond had said. And it gave Ernie himself a brilliant idea too. "We could wear mustaches," Ernie suggested, pointing at the poster.

Amazing Desmond sprang from his seat and clapped Ernie on the shoulder. "I always knew you were extraordinary," he crowed.

"Of course, it was I who discovered him," Super Whiz added modestly.

"Great work, partner," Maud agreed.

Ernie felt himself turning pink with pleasure.

"I'm sure we must have some mustaches somewhere," Desmond said. He hurried to the storeroom and started rummaging among the costumes and boots. "Aha! I thought so . . ." He came back carrying a hand mirror and a shoebox marked "Mustaches and Miscellaneous Facial Hair" and put them on the table.

Ernie reached into the box and pulled out a selection of mustaches for himself and Maud to try. He held up a bristly gray one and a narrow black one before settling on a bushy brown mustache.

"I look so old," he said, admiring himself in the mirror. "Like a teenager."

Maud's long black mustache curled up at the tips. She looked at herself for several seconds in the mirror Ernie held up for her. "You don't think it makes me look like lamb dressed as mutton?" she asked anxiously.

"You look very dignified," Ernie assured her. "There's no way Pencil Pete would recognize us in these disguises." Then something occurred to him. "But what if the judges don't recognize us either?"

"Excuse me?" said Super Whiz. At the other

end of the table, he and Amazing Desmond were trying out disguises too. Desmond was wearing glasses and a false nose as well as a mustache, while Super Whiz now sported a long black beard.

"How do we look?" said Desmond, tweaking his new nose.

"Wow," Ernie said. "I never would have known it was you."

"That's the idea," said Desmond. "What was that you were saying about the judges?"

Ernie explained his fear. "If the judges of the

Heroes of the Year award come to Baxter to do their inspection today, they'll think Maud and I are neglecting our patrol." He looked regretfully at the golden trophy on the shelf, then shook his head. "But Baxter needs us," he said, standing up.

Amazing Desmond looked at him for a moment then whispered something to Super Whiz, who nodded.

"Off you go then," Desmond said to Ernie and Maud. "And good luck."

Taking a deep breath, Ernie opened the door and stepped outside. He felt rather nervous about walking down Main Street in disguise. What if he saw someone he knew? He'd have to ignore them. He patted the bristles on his upper lip. "Is my mustache on straight?" he asked Maud.

"Sure is, partner. What about mine?"

Ernie adjusted Maud's mustache, which had slipped a bit, and then they set off.

They spent the morning pacing along Main Street, then they bought sandwiches for lunch as usual and ate them in the park before resuming their patrol.

As they were walking past the bookstore, Ernie heard someone tapping on the window. When he peered through the glass, he saw the bookstore owner waving to them.

"I think Mrs. Lee wants to talk to us, Maud," Ernie said. He led the way into the bookstore and walked up to the counter where Mrs. Lee stood.

"Oh, I'm sorry." Mrs. Lee looked confused. "I thought you were someone else. Who are you?" Now that Ernie was standing in front of her, she clearly didn't recognize him with his mustache.

"It's me," Ernie began, then stopped. A master of disguise wouldn't use his real name, he realized. And even though he liked Mrs. Lee, he couldn't risk revealing his identity.

"He's Excellent Egbert," said a gruff voice beside him. "And I'm Mysterious Manfred."

Ernie turned to see that Maud had jumped up so that her woolly chin rested on the counter.

"Excellent Egbert and Mysterious Manfred," Mrs. Lee repeated. "That's funny. I've never heard those names before. But you do look familiar . . ." She was staring at Maud. "You're not a sheep, are you?"

Ernie froze, but Maud didn't falter.

"A sheep?" she said indignantly. "How could you say such a thing? Since when do sheep have mustaches?"

Mrs. Lee blushed. "My mistake," she apologized.

"That's quite all right," said Ernie politely, and

he and Maud returned to Main Street.

"These disguises must be really good if Mrs. Lee didn't recognize us," Ernie observed. "But we've been patrolling in our disguises all day, and we haven't spotted Pencil Pete once."

"Maybe the sight of us in our disguises has scared him away from Baxter completely," Maud suggested.

"It's possible, I suppose," said Ernie. "But if

we've scared him away from Baxter that means he's on his way to another town to cause chaos there. I want him to leave Baxter, but not if it means he'll be wreaking havoc in another community. Maybe the disguises were a bad idea."

"I see what you mean, partner," Maud agreed. "Let's go ask Super Whiz and Amazing Desmond what they think."

# SIX

When they walked through the door of 32 Main Street, Ernie and Maud found Amazing Desmond and Super Whiz in a panic. "Quick, everyone, remove your disguises," Super Whiz ordered.

Ernie was about to ask why, but Super Whiz looked so frightened that he decided just to do as he was told.

Ouch! Ernie's skin burned as he ripped the mustache from his upper lip. He had just kneeled beside Maud, who was having trouble tearing her long black mustache free of her fleece, when the door was flung open.

Valiant Vera stalked into the room. "So it *was* you," she said, her eyes blazing as they raked over Amazing Desmond, who was clutching the box marked "Mustaches and Miscellaneous Facial Hair," and Super Whiz, who still held the long black beard in one hand. Ernie had never seen Vera so angry.

"Ah, Vera, good afternoon," said Super Whiz, but his normally officious tone sounded a bit forced.

"How're things in Beezerville?" Desmond asked innocently.

"Things in Beezerville are fine," Vera snapped. "But I'm not so sure about Baxter. If you put as much effort into your superhero work as you did into cheating, you'd probably win. When I saw you trying to deceive other superheroes with those disguises . . ." She shook her head in disgust.

"What . . . what happened?" Ernie asked hesitantly.

Vera looked at the bushy brown mustache in Ernie's hand and the long black mustache dangling from Maud's woolly cheek. "I don't know what role you two played in this fiasco, but you'd better have a very good explanation for those mustaches you're holding," she growled.

"Ernie and Maud had nothing to do with it," Desmond assured Vera hurriedly.

Nothing to do with what? Ernie wondered. "Maud and I were trying to fool Pencil Pete by wearing disguises," he said, and quickly outlined their plan. "But we didn't see him all day, so we

were wondering if we needed a new plan. We just came back here for some advice."

Valiant Vera's expression softened. "Your plan sounds like a very good one, Ernie," she said. "I'm sorry it didn't work. But if it's advice you're seeking, there's no use asking these two. Marj and I were over at National Headquarters in the city, and what do you think we saw? Desmond and Super Whiz at the information desk, asking when the Heroes of the Year judges were going to be in Baxter!"

Super Whiz and Amazing Desmond, looking embarrassed, were staring at the floor.

"But, Vera," said Desmond, "what were you and Marj doing at National Headquarters? You never mentioned you were going there."

For a moment, it was Vera's turn to look embarrassed.

"I had a meeting with Stupendous Sue," she murmured.

"A meeting with Stupendous Sue?" At the mention of the Superheroes Society's national president Super Whiz's head shot up. "What about?"

Vera's lips tightened. Then she said, "Well, if you must know, Stupendous Sue offered me a job. At the time I turned it down — but now . . ." She looked at her colleagues. "I've changed my mind. Clearly I don't belong in Baxter anymore."

Ernie's mouth dropped open. The other superheroes were looking equally stunned. Even Housecat Woman was sitting up in her chair, her eyes wide.

Valiant Vera was leaving Baxter Branch!

# SEVEN

"I'd better get packing, then," Valiant Vera said into the shocked silence.

"Vera, wait," Amazing Desmond began. "I can explain." But he was interrupted by an urgent pounding at the door.

Super Whiz strode across the room and opened it to reveal a dark-haired man in an apron and chef's hat. He was clutching a menu and was clearly distressed.

"Ronald!" Desmond said. "What's wrong?"

"This is wrong!" cried Ronald, waving the menu.

"Ooh, is that the new menu?" Desmond said. He snatched it from the pizza chef's grasp and studied it eagerly. "Ronald," he said, looking at the picture of a smiling Ronald, "no offense, but that mustache doesn't really suit you."

"I don't have a mustache!" Ronald howled in anguish. "A funny little man in a blue suit ran into my restaurant a few minutes ago and drew mustaches on all my menus."

The superheroes gasped.

"Pencil Pete did this?" Amazing Desmond said. "Quick, Ronald, which way did he go?"

"Toward the town hall," said Ronald. "Carrying a pencil!"

The superheroes bolted for the door. Ernie took off up Main Street. His cape streamed behind him as he pounded along the pavement, running faster than he had ever run before. This time, he would catch Pencil Pete. He wouldn't let Baxter down.

A clattering behind him told him that Maud was at his heels.

"I can't see where Pencil Pete has gone," Ernie

said in frustration. "Can you, Maud?"

They both looked left and right, then — "There!" shouted Maud, and she led the way across the crosswalk.

As she cantered toward the fruit shop, Ernie saw a small man in a blue suit squeezing between the apples and bananas.

"Maud, watch out!" he called in alarm as the displays began to teeter. "The bananas!"

But Maud was already skidding up the pavement, a banana squashed beneath each hoof. She sailed right past Pencil Pete, slid into a lamppost, and began to spin.

"H-h-help!" she bleated as her left hooves went one way and her right hooves went the other.

Pelting up the sidewalk behind Pencil Pete, Ernie saw that the look on his sidekick's face was one of pure terror as she sat immobile on the sidewalk, her legs splayed, and the pencil-wielding wrongdoer drawing nearer and nearer.

"Maud!" Ernie cried as the realization struck him. "Maud, you're doing the splits!"

As his words sank in, Maud's terrified

expression turned to determination. Ernie knew what she was thinking: sheep can do anything!

Pencil Pete, meanwhile, on observing the sheep in the red leotard doing the splits, stopped dead in his tracks. As Pencil Pete gaped in disbelief at Maud, Ernie reached over and snatched the enormous pencil from his hand.

"Halt, you evil villain!" It was Amazing Desmond's voice. Valiant Vera was close behind, and Super Whiz was limping after them, one foot stuck in a melon.

The man in the blue suit turned to face them. The first thing Ernie noticed about Pencil Pete was the mustache hanging across his upper lip like a furry caterpillar.

"Evil villain? Me?" Pencil Pete sounded genuinely surprised.

"Yes, you!" thundered Amazing Desmond. He held up Ronald's menu. "Look what you've done to poor Ronald here."

"And the mayor," Super Whiz added sternly, pointing in the direction of the town hall.

Pencil Pete looked from the menu to the town hall and smiled. "Don't they look wonderful?" he said.

"Wonderful?" sputtered Super Whiz.

"Of course," said Pencil Pete. "I'm a mustache salesman," he explained. "I think mustaches make people look extremely distinguished." He smoothed his furry mustache proudly. He pointed to the picture of the mayor. "I think she looks *better* with a mustache."

"Me too," said Desmond, then clapped a hand over his mouth as Vera fixed him with a severe look.

"I think you'd better come back to our headquarters," Vera said to Pencil Pete. "We're going to give you a box of erasers and a good talking-to."

Desmond and Super Whiz led Pencil Pete away.

"Did you see that sheep?" Pencil Pete was asking. "She was doing the splits!"

Vera turned to Ernie and Maud.

"Well done, you two," she said, as Ernie put his arms around Maud's middle and pulled until she was standing on all four hooves once more. "You leapt into action to protect your community. That's good superheroing. And, Ernie, that was quite a sprint — I don't think I've ever seen a boy run so fast. Extraordinary. As for you, Maud . . ."

Valiant Vera shook her head. "I've never seen a sheep do the splits before, but I'm not surprised. I don't think there's anything you can't do, Marvelous Maud."

"Valiant Vera . . ." said Ernie. There was a lump in his throat so big he could hardly speak. Even though they had caught Pencil Pete, he felt miserable. "Are you really leaving Baxter?" he choked out finally.

Vera looked at him thoughtfully. "We'll see, Ernie. We'll see."

# EIGHT

The sun was beaming down as Ernie hurried along Main Street on a Monday afternoon three weeks later. His cape was pressed and his boots were polished to a high shine.

Maud was waiting for him under the town hall clock. She wasn't wearing her leotard, but her pink cape snapped crisply in the breeze as she and Ernie made their way to number 32.

Ernie glanced over his shoulder at the picture of the mayor on the town hall. She no longer had a mustache. The superheroes of Baxter Branch had explained to Pencil Pete that people should

be allowed to decide for themselves whether mustaches made them look better, and Pete had agreed to erase all the mustaches he had drawn.

Then Super Whiz and Amazing Desmond had explained that they weren't intending to cheat when they went to the National Headquarters in disguise. They told Vera how Ernie had worried that the judges of the Heroes of the Year award wouldn't recognize him in his disguise — but how he had decided that saving Baxter from Pencil Pete was more important than winning the trophy. They had been hoping that if they could find out who the judges were, they could explain to them that Ernie and Maud were patrolling in disguise, and why. They had decided to wear disguises themselves so that it wouldn't appear as if the superheroes of Baxter were trying to influence the judges' decision in favor of their own trainees.

Valiant Vera didn't think that their plan was a very good one, but she agreed that Super Whiz and Amazing Desmond had had the best interests of Ernie and Maud at heart. She even apologized

to Desmond and Super Whiz for having assumed they were cheating.

After all the explaining had been done, the superheroes of Baxter Branch drank lemonade to celebrate Ernie and Maud stopping Pencil Pete, as well as Super Whiz and Desmond's teamwork (for as Vera pointed out, they hadn't bickered once all day), and Valiant Vera's decision to stay in Baxter.

Now, as he pushed open the door of number 32, Ernie was still smiling at the memory. But his heart nearly stopped beating when he and Maud were greeted with a loud chorus of "Hooray for Extraordinary Ernie! Hooray for Marvelous Maud!"

The room was full of people, all cheering for him and Maud.

With rising excitement he asked, "Have we won? Are we the Heroes of the Year?"

"No," said Valiant Vera. "The Heroes of the Year are Mei-Li and Cuddles from Beezerville."

"Oh," said Ernie, trying to hide his disappointment. "I mean, that's great. They really

deserve it."

"But the Superheroes Society National Head-quarters has received so many letters from the community about the fine work you two have been doing in Baxter that you've been given honorable mentions," Vera said.

"Ahem," said Super Whiz.

"Please, Whiz, no speeches," Amazing Desmond said. "The pizza will get cold."

Super Whiz shot Desmond a furious look, then said, "As president of the Baxter Branch of the Superheroes Society, it is my great privilege to present these ribbons. Marvelous Maud, through your outstanding gymnastics you succeeded in stopping evil in its tracks. (Though, of course, Pencil Pete turned out to be misguided rather than evil.) Well done."

Maud trotted forward and stood with her eyes shining as Super Whiz fixed a silver ribbon to her fleecy chest.

"And Extraordinary Ernie, you are honored for your sensational show of speed and your superhero spirit. Congratulations!"

Ernie stepped forward, and as Super Whiz pinned the ribbon to his chest he thought he would burst with pride and happiness.

"Now let the party begin!" whooped Amazing Desmond, and everyone cheered again.

For quite a while, Ernie and Maud were caught up in the crowd of well-wishers who pressed forward to shake their hands (and hooves). But finally they managed to get to the long table in the center of the room, which was groaning under the weight of several enormous pizzas. They helped themselves to a slice of the vegetarian special.

Amazing Desmond and Ronald were standing nearby.

"And so in gratitude," the pizza chef was saying, "I have named this Super-Quadruple-Supremo Supreme with extra cheese and pepperoni . . . 'the Desmond'."

Desmond, Ernie noticed, was blinking back tears of joy.

Super Whiz was sitting at the far end of the long table, signing copies of *100 Handy Hints for Heroing* for Mrs. Lee, who wanted to sell them in her shop.

Even Pencil Pete was at the party, holding the shoebox of "Mustaches and Miscellaneous Facial Hair" in one hand, and a mirror in the other.

"I see what you mean," the mayor was saying as she held a neat black mustache to her upper lip and peered at herself in the mirror. "It does make me look very distinguished. I'd like to order one

just like this."

"Letting people try on mustaches for them-selves really works," Pete said. "I should have been carrying a sample box rather than drawing mustaches on pictures."

Ernie continued to scan the crowd until finally he spotted Valiant Vera sitting on the arm of Housecat Woman's chair. Housecat Woman was curled into a tight ball, and had one arm curved over her head as if she was trying to block out the noise of the party.

"Valiant Vera," Super Whiz called to her, "you never told us what job you were offered by Stupendous Sue."

Valiant Vera smiled. "Sue asked Marjory and me to judge the Heroes of the Year award," she replied. "But I told her I wasn't interested."

"You turned down a senior position at National Headquarters?" Super Whiz said in astonishment.

Vera shrugged. "I like it here in Baxter."

Ernie smiled. He was glad to hear it. He turned to his sidekick. "How are your classes going, Maud?" he asked.

"My teacher says she's never seen a sheep so flexible," Maud told him. "I'm thinking about giving up gymnastics, though."

"Why?" Ernie asked. "You're proving that a sheep can do anything."

"That's true, Ernie," said Maud. "But I've decided I'd like to focus all my efforts on being the

best superhero I can be."

"Me too," said Ernie. As he raised a hand to touch the silver ribbon on his chest, he knew that being a superhero was better than all the trophies and ribbons and awards in the world.

# Acknowledgments

I'd like to award big gold Heroes of the Year trophies to Tegan Morrison and Chren Byng, and silver medallions to the mustachioed marvels of bookselling and HarperCollins Australia who so graciously donated their upper lips on request.

*F.W.*

Fearless Frances & friend

# About the author

As well as the Ernie & Maud series, Fearless **Frances Watts** is the author of *The Song of the Winns* and *The Spies of Gerander*, from the Gerander trilogy. She has also written picture books *Kisses for Daddy, Parsley Rabbit's Book about Books, Captain Crabclaw's Crew, A Rat in a Stripy Sock,* and her first picture book with Judy Watson, *Goodnight, Mice!* — which, oddly, doesn't feature a single sheep.

Although her natural superpower has not yet emerged, she did once rescue a horse from a fire.

Jittery Judy & friend

# About the illustrator

Jittery **Judy Watson** would like to state that she did not scribble that mustache on Fearless Frances. She has been much too busy drawing proper pictures for books like the Ernie & Maud series and *Goodnight, Mice!*

By the way, Jittery Judy thinks that Fearless Frances's new costume is lovely, even if the undies *are* on the outside. Not sure if her horse agrees.

Also available

## Extraordinary Ernie & Marvelous Maud

Ernie Eggers is thrilled when he wins a superhero contest and becomes Extraordinary Ernie (after school on Mondays, Tuesdays, and Thursdays, and all day Saturday). But his excitement turns to dismay when he discovers that his sidekick is a sheep. It doesn't take him long to realize, though, that there has never been another sheep quite like Marvelous Maud.

Ernie & Maud

## The Middle Sheep

The adventures of Extraordinary Ernie and Marvelous Maud continue . . . but what — or *who* — is making the usually cheerful and dependable Maud so grumpy? And why are she and Ernie arguing all the time? It seems to Ernie that being his sidekick just isn't important to Maud anymore. Then Valiant Vera says that if the two trainee superheroes can't work together, they will be thrown out of the Superheroes Society! Ernie and Maud must learn the value of teamwork (and how to get a sheep out of a tree) before it's too late.

Ernie & Maud

## The Greatest Sheep in History

Ernie and Maud are thrilled to be attending the National Superheroes Conference with the other superheroes from Baxter. But when the conference is disrupted by Chicken George — the most terrifying and villainous chicken anyone has ever seen — it will take more than just an ordinary superhero to save the day.